CB137248

The William Shakespeare

CHILDREN'S COLLECTION

Dados Internacionais de Catalogação na Publicação (CIP) de acordo com ISBD

S527a Shakespeare, William
All's Well That Ends Well / William Shakespeare. - Jandira, SP : W. Books, 2025.
104 p. ; 12,80cm x 19,80cm. - (Classics).

ISBN: 978-65-5294-207-4

1. Literatura inglesa. 2. Clássicos. 3. Aventura. 4. Fantasia. 5. Imaginação. I. Título.
II. Série.

2025-2506 CDD 823
CDU 821.111

Elaborada por Lucio Feitosa - CRB-8/8803
Índice para catálogo sistemático:
1. Literatura inglesa : 823
2. Literatura inglesa : 821.111-31

Text based on the original play by William Shakespeare,
adapted by Georgina Brown
Illustrations by Mai Ngo

1st edition in 2025
www.cirandacultural.com.br

EASY CLASSICS

William Shakespeare

All's Well That Ends Well

W. Books

Helena

An orphan who lives under the protection of the Countess of Roussillon

Diana and her mother

A young woman and her widowed mother

Bertram

The Count of Roussillon

Parolles
A soldier and Bertram's boastful friend

Countess
The Countess of Roussillon, noble woman and mother of Bertram

King of France
A powerful monarch of France

Lafeu
Noble lord and advisor to the King of France

Chapter One

Turning away from her son, the countess stared out of the window with sadness in her eyes. 'I can't believe I am losing my son so soon after my husband's death!' she uttered glumly. Bertram joined her at the window. He placed his arm gently around her and gazed out at the beautiful rural countryside of Roussillon.

'I feel the same way, Mother. I miss Father and I'll miss you dearly. But I must serve the king,' he explained gently.

Lafeu stepped closer. 'The king will treat you like a son and look after you. He has always loved your family,' he reassured them.

'How likely is it that he will recover?' the countess asked, knowing that the king's health was getting worse.

Lafeu shook his head, sadly. 'He has given up hope,' he replied.

'If only your father were here, Helena,' the countess declared, speaking to a young girl standing quietly in the corner. ‘Gerard could heal anyone,’ she added, moving over to wipe tears from Helena’s cheek. ‘Helena is smart like him. I have high hopes for this sweet girl,’ she said, squeezing her hand gently.

Lafeu nodded from across the room, already aware of the great reputation of Helena's father.

Bertram looked at his mother and stood waiting. After a moment she said, 'Okay, you have my blessing. Go. You are so much like your father. Don't talk too much, but be strong. Look after yourself. Love all, trust a few.' She shot a look at Parolles, who was waiting across the room. She hugged her son goodbye.

Helena watched silently. She was grateful that Bertram would have company, but knew his friend Parolles was a coward and a fool who would not provide much protection. She nodded goodbye as the others left her alone.

Her sobs grew louder. She dared not share the real reason for her tears. The countess believed that Helena still mourned her father, though in truth she was broken-hearted. She loved Bertram, but knowing she would never be a suitable match upset her. She needed a plan.

After a long journey, the three men arrived at the king's palace.

mourning
The feeling and expression of great sadness that follows a death.

The king was unenthusiastically discussing events with his lords. 'The Italians are at war again. My good friend the King of Austria has said we should not support the Duke of Florence with this battle, so we won't,' he began. 'But if our French soldiers want to fight, they can pick their sides,' he added, dismissively.

There was a knock on the door. A steward entered and introduced Bertram and the two other men walking behind him.

Florence

A city in Italy. In Shakespeare's time, Florence was one of the most important cities in the world. A Florentine is someone who comes from Florence.

'Bertram. Welcome to Paris! How much you look like your father,' the king declared, smiling fondly as Bertram bowed and pledged his service. He looked closely at the young man's face. 'Oh, to be young. I wish I was as youthful as when your father and I first became soldiers. He was such a good man, so brave and successful, yet he treated everyone he met with the same respect. Such a great loss,' the king offered, sincerely. 'I heard he had the best care. His doctor may have been able to give me a little longer,' he muttered, forcing a smile.

Bertram nodded in agreement and thanked the king once again for welcoming him so kindly.

Chapter Two

Back in Roussillon, a steward was telling the countess that she had accidentally overheard Helena say that she was in love with Bertram. She explained how sad Helena had sounded, since she knew they could never be together because of her social status. The countess listened, saddened to hear about Helena's pain but not surprised by the news. She'd always suspected it. She asked the steward to fetch Helena.

As Helena entered the room, the countess watched her closely. Helena's eyes were red and her cheeks flushed. Her body language spoke volumes.

'Dearest Helena. Come here. You are like a daughter to me and I consider myself your mother,' the countess said, waiting for Helena's response. She noticed her awkward expression and probed further. 'Do you not see me as your mother?'

Helena kept her eyes fixed on the floor and replied, 'I would be honoured for you to be my mother, but that would make the count my brother. You are all noble people and I come from nothing. I could never be your daughter.'

'Perhaps my daughter-in-law,' the countess chanced. Seeing

Helena's eyes light up, she added, 'Tell me the truth. Do you love my son?'

Helena started to protest, but gave in. 'Please. Don't be angry. I love him but don't expect

anything from him. I know I'm not deserving of him and don't know how I ever could be.' She looked at the countess. 'Though I have a plan,' she revealed.

'You wish to go to Paris?' the countess guessed.

Helena nodded. 'Your son leaving gave me the idea. I have my father's medicines and I truly believe I can help the king!' she declared, boldly. Noticing

the countess's doubtful look, she continued, 'With my father's reputation and your blessing, the king might give me a chance.'

The countess smiled and looked into Helena's eyes. 'Go, brilliant Helena. I'll pray for you. Good luck!'

The royal court buzzed with activity; the king was saying farewell to his noblemen as they left for war. Bertram watched, upset that he had been requested to stay at the palace because of his age. He did his best to give words of encouragement to the noblemen, even suggesting that he may sneak away to join them.

Boasting of his own experiences of war, Parolles encouraged Bertram, insisting he should go and fight bravely if he felt strongly about it.

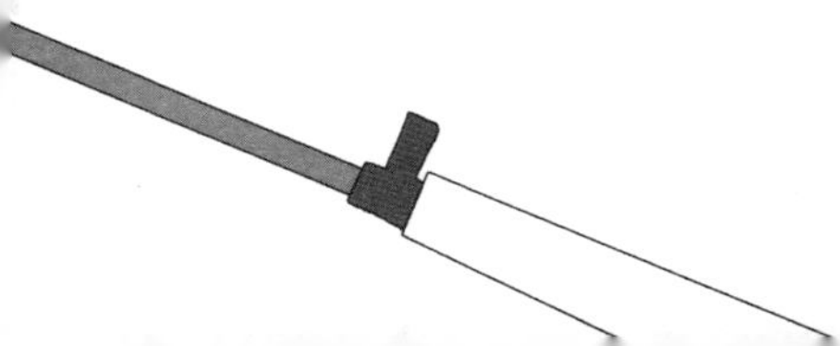

Bursting into the king's room, Lafeu excitedly announced the surprise arrival of Helena. The king looked bewildered. 'What is it you want?' he asked, as Helena shyly entered.

'My father was Gerard de Carbon, a brilliant doctor. I have come here because he left me his medicines, and I believe there is one that will completely heal you,' she announced, trying hard to be brave.

The king nodded. 'I knew him.

It's very kind of you to come here. But the doctors have said nothing can be done.' He turned to leave.

With one last attempt, Helena suggested, 'What is the worst that could happen? I bet my life I can heal you.'

The king considered the offer. 'Okay. I suppose you are right – it's worth a try. But what do you want from me?' he asked.

Helena thought for a moment. 'I want a husband. I wish to marry someone of my choice from the royal bloodline,' she requested confidently.

Not truly believing that anything could be done, the king agreed to the terms, and they came up with a plan of action.

Chapter Three

There was a commotion at the king's palace. Excited whispers filled the corridors. Lafeu paced with his hands on his head, eyebrows dipped. 'It's a miracle! Our doctors had all given up hope. "Incurable," they said,' he muttered in shock. Bertram and Parolles agreed, equally amazed.

'It is strange,' Parolles began,

commotion

A noisy confusion.

his voice filled with curiosity. 'Who'd have thought? This can't be ignored. It's clearly the work of–'

'It is a miracle!' Lafeu interrupted. 'It is clear that this girl has been picked by the grace of heaven to do powerful work,' he concluded. The others nodded, refusing to believe that there was another explanation.

Footsteps approached. The king entered with Helena. He beamed and called for the lords to assemble. Once they'd all gathered, he said to Helena, 'These men are like my sons. I have the power as king to make choices for them. So, Helena, choose one of these noble men and they will not refuse.'

Helena walked around slowly, examining each of the men. Finally, she reached Bertram. 'I choose you. I offer my service and life to you,' she said, smiling.

The king patted Bertram on the back. 'Well, that's settled. You shall have lovely Helena as your wife!'

Confusion and objection spread on Bertram's face. 'My wife? I cannot marry her. She grew up in my father's court. A poor doctor's daughter! I'm a nobleman, so I cannot marry someone of such low status!' he argued angrily.

As his words spilt out, the king's face turned a dark shade of red. He marched towards Bertram. 'You think you are too good for her? How dare you. You don't like

her because she has no title?' he huffed. 'Well, let me tell you this. When people do good things, they earn their status, they gain their title. They are raised up.' He stepped closer to Bertram. 'People who are born with titles aren't automatically gifted with honour. Honour is earned, not inherited! She is young, wise and beautiful. You are young, foolish and entitled!' he roared.

Bertram simply shook his head.

Helena lightly touched the king's

arm. 'It's okay. I'm just glad that I could help you get better,' she whispered, turning to leave.

The king erupted with fury. 'No! I made a promise. Bertram, you'll marry Helena otherwise it's your honour at risk. I'm the king. I have the power to change someone's status for better and for worse. Helena will be given a noble status and wealth, but you will be released from my protection. I'll always remember how you shunned me,' he warned.

Bertram's attitude shifted. 'Of course, Your Majesty. I now realise that I was wrong.' He took Helena's hand. 'I'll marry Helena if that is who you pick for me,' he agreed.

At this, the king clapped his hands. 'Excellent! The ceremony will take place tonight!

We shall have a feast.' He scooped up Helena and left, the others following behind. Lafeu shot Parolles a satisfied grin, and Parolles shook his head in annoyance.

Bertram sulked over to Parolles. 'I'm not doing it. I'm not marrying her. I'm going to run away to the Tuscan war,' he revealed.

Parolles's face lit up. 'Yes. Let's do it. A far more honourable way to live!' he declared.

With a final nod, Bertram decided to let his mother and the king know of his plan by letter,

once he had escaped. They hurried to Bertram's room to get ready and discuss their next steps.

Chapter Four

A short while later, Parolles found Helena and gave her the message from Bertram that they had concocted. 'My lord has been called away on work tonight. He must leave immediately. He's sorry to leave on your wedding day, but he will be back soon,' he lied.

'I understand,' Helena murmured, dropping her head.

concoct

To imagine or invent something that may not be true.

'He'd also like you to tell the king that you must leave for your own reasons immediately,' Parolles explained, avoiding eye contact.

Helena nodded. 'Anything else?'

Parolles was already leaving. 'No, I'll tell him you've understood,' he called, his voice trailing off.

With glassy eyes, Helena watched as he dashed away, wondering what reason she could give the king.

In a nearby room, Lafeu tried

his best to warn Bertram that Parolles wasn't to be trusted. 'You know he isn't a real solider, don't you?' he urged, keeping his voice low.

Bertram defended Parolles,

claiming he was a brave soldier. Before Lafeu could respond, Parolles burst into the room. Lafeu greeted him, unimpressed, and wished Bertram luck. He warned him to be careful with whom he trusted.

'What did you do to annoy him?' Bertram asked when Lafeu was out of earshot.

Parolles shrugged his shoulders. 'It's done, sir. Helena has gone to speak to the king and will leave shortly,' he whispered.

Bertram smiled. A faint noise in the doorway made them look up. Helena cautiously peeked in, and Bertram signalled for her to enter.

'I've spoken to the king. He's given permission for me to leave, but would like to speak to you,' she said, fiddling with a special ring the king had given her as a token of his appreciation.

Bertram drew closer to Helena. 'I'm sorry to leave so soon, but it is for important duties. Send this ahead to my mother and I'll join you soon.' He passed her a letter and guided her to the door. 'Now,

go. I must leave soon. Goodbye for now,' he said, gently steering her out the door and closing it.

Helena stood alone in the corridor, unsure of what had happened.

Bertram and Parolles listened at the door until they heard Helena leave. 'Let's go. Off to war!' Parolles cheered.

Meanwhile, in Roussillon, the countess eagerly awaited news from her son and Helena. When a steward burst in clutching a letter, the countess could barely contain her excitement. 'Quickly! Read it,' she instructed.

'I have sent you a daughter-in-law. She has healed the king,' the letter began. The countess clapped her hands with glee. The steward continued, 'She has ruined me. I have run away and will stay away. I wanted you to know first. Your unfortunate son, Bertram.' The steward

finished reading and looked at the ground in embarrassment.

The countess stared into the

distance, remaining silent for a minute. 'What has he done? He's mistreated a lovely, honourable girl. He'll lose the respect of the king!' she exclaimed.

Suddenly, there was an

announcement that two gentlemen and Helena had arrived. Seeing Helena's sadness as they entered, the countess went to comfort her.

'He's gone,' Helena said, unhappily.

The countess turned to the gentlemen. 'Where is my son?' she asked.

'We met him on the way. He's gone to serve the Duke of Florence,' they reported.

Her eyes widened. 'To be a

soldier? Who's he with? Parolles?' she demanded. The gentlemen nodded. 'I knew it! He's a terrible influence on Bertram. Will you deliver a letter?' she asked. They nodded and followed the countess out of the room.

Once again, Helena found herself alone. 'He says he has nothing in France to stay for. He says that we must exchange rings to truly be husband and wife. But he has gone. Am I that bad that I've driven him to war?

He's in danger because of me. I'll leave. If I go, he may return,' she murmured to herself. She took a final look around and left.

Chapter Five

Trumpets blared on the battlefield. The Duke of Florence called to Bertram amidst the noise, 'You're our commander now! Lead the cavalry. We trust in you!'

Bertram sat upright in his saddle, adjusting his posture. 'I am honoured by the title and will strive to make you proud,' he replied, preparing for battle. With the growing sound of drums, he signalled for the others to follow and rode courageously into the fight.

Back in Roussillon, the countess was close to tears. 'She's gone?' she asked, getting the steward to reread Helena's letter. Her heart ached as she listened.

The letter said: 'My love for a man far more honourable than myself has caused so much pain. I will leave so he can return. Please inform my dearest husband that he can come back from war as soon as

possible and live in peace. It's all my fault.'

Helena's sad words hung in the air.

'Poor angel. She deserves better. Someone who truly values her. Write to Bertram and tell him she's left. Hopefully he'll return, and then Helena too. I love them both dearly, but he must realise he's made a huge mistake!' she instructed. As the steward rushed off, the countess took a seat, exhausted from the whirlwind of emotions she had experienced.

Peering out of a window in Florence, a group of women watched as the troops marched towards the city. 'I've heard that the French count has served very well,' one woman said.

'Yes. They say he captured the commander! But beware of these men. I have told our neighbour how you were approached by the earl's friend. What was his name?' the older lady asked.

'Parolles. A horrible man. Trying to win over girls with gifts and promises. All lies!' replied another in disgust.

Outside, Helena, dressed as a pilgrim, approached the house. The ladies moved from the window to welcome her.

'Hello, good pilgrim. Where are you heading?' one asked as she opened the door. Helena greeted them with a smile and told them she planned to go to the pilgrimage site of Saint Jacques le Grand. The older lady told her about an inn she could stay in.

pilgrim

A person who travels to foreign lands to visit places of great or religious importance.

As Helena turned to leave, the sound of drums could be heard, coming from the hills.

'They're coming back,' the lady said to Helena. 'You sound like you're from France? Some of your countrymen are coming by. The Count Roussillon. Do you know him?' she asked.

Helena's heart skipped a beat at the mention of his name. All she could do was nod.

'Apparently the king made him marry a bride he didn't like, so he ran away. Do you think that is true?' one of the younger ladies asked eagerly.

'It is. I know his wife and she is of low status. Not worthy of such a great man,' Helena said, her voice steady.

One of the women laughed. 'Not worthy? Bah! He's been acting dishonourably. Trying to win over this one,' she said, pointing to a girl standing behind her. They all shook their heads.

'It's probably because his vile

worthy

A person who has value or is honourable; someone who deserves respect.

friend encouraged him to, but I'm ready to reject them all,' the girl claimed boldly. Although the words cut through Helena, she hid her pain and agreed to join the women for dinner.

Back at the soldiers' camp, two Florentine soldiers were talking to Bertram in hushed voices. 'He lies, your lordship. He is not what he says. Let's test him so you can see what a coward and liar he is!' one of them insisted.

Bertram was beginning to have doubts. This was one of many warnings he had received about Parolles. 'How would we test him though?' he asked.

One of the soldiers thought for a moment. 'Ask him to take back the drum he lost. He keeps boasting he'll go. While he's away pretending, we'll capture him. We'll pretend to be the enemy and ask him to betray you. He'll do it the instant he's caught. You wait.'

The others smiled, pleased with the plan.

betray

To break a person's trust or not be loyal, especially by giving their enemies information.

Chapter Six

After spending the evening with the ladies she'd met earlier, Helena decided to speak truthfully with the older woman. In the humble home filled with welcoming smells and soft lights, they'd laughed and shared stories of their encounters with fools. Now, she prepared to tell her the truth. Helena took a bag of gold from her pocket and put it on the table.

'I have something that I

must tell you,' she began. The woman's eyes remained fixed on the gold. 'I am the count's wife. I need your help with something, and I apologise for having to ask, but I'm willing to pay for your assistance.' She pushed the bag towards the woman.

'I can prove my truthfulness with this wealth. All I want is for your daughter to ask him for his ring. It is a family heirloom,' she explained. 'And then, give him this one in exchange,' she said, removing the ring that the king had given her. 'Exchanging the rings will make our marriage official and he will accept me as his wife.'

The lady seemed to understand and considered the plan. When Helena offered her another bag of gold, the lady agreed that when Bertram came to see her daughter, Diana, she would persuade him to part with his ring and swap it for the king's.

Hiding in the bushes, several Florentine soldiers were waiting to ambush Parolles, while the leader explained their plan. 'This is the only route. When you see him, make sure you sound awful. Speak in a garbled language. He will never know it's not the real thing. We'll claim only one of us can interpret his language. We'll pretend to talk to each other and he'll never know.'

A branch snapping underfoot hushed their voices. It was Parolles.

'A couple of hours should do it,' he said to himself. 'I'll pretend I was captured, tear my clothes, break my sword.' The hidden group listened, chuckling about his foolishness.

Parolles continued to speak aloud, 'If only I had an enemy's drum. I could say I stole it back!' He abruptly stopped talking.

The *BOOM* of a nearby drum had made him freeze with fear.

The *BOOMS* grew louder as the soldiers leapt from the bushes, garbling aggressively in their made-up language. As one of them blindfolded him, Parolles pleaded, 'Does anyone understand me? I must speak with you. I'll provide secrets that will ruin the Florentines!'

The group grinned at each other. Slowly, the leader responded. 'I understand you. We'll give you an audience. But you must tell the truth or pay with your life,' he told

a scared Parolles.

Trembling, Parolles swore to share all of the army's secrets if they let him live. The leader whispered to a soldier to run ahead and tell Bertram of their success. The group silently laughed, watching Parolles squirm.

Across the city, Bertram tried his best to impress Diana. She reminded him that he was married, to which he scoffed. 'We have spoken about this.

I was forced to marry her. I love you. I'll be faithful to you,' he claimed, keeping his voice low.

Diana laughed. 'You'll be faithful, you say. Prove it. Give me your ring. Show me that you are being truthful.' She stared into his eyes, determined.

Bertram seemed hesitant. 'This ring has been passed through my family for centuries. I–' he started, but Diana maintained her intense gaze. Reluctantly, he handed her the ring. She promised

reluctant

Not eager or willing to do something.

she would return it later, once she could trust his word. Bertram left happy, convinced he had won her over. Diana, however, was contemplating the next stage of the plan.

contemplate

To spend time thinking about something carefully.

Chapter Seven

Two soldiers were eagerly waiting for Bertram's return. 'Did you give him the letter from his mother?' one asked.

The other soldier nodded and said, 'There was something that upset him as he read it.' They gossiped about Bertram's actions and discussed the trouble he was in with the king. 'He'll ruin himself,' they agreed.

'We'll wait till he gets here then

we shall question Parolles,' they decided.

A nearby soldier who'd been listening approached them. 'Have you heard news of the war? It seems that peace has finally been made. Do you think the count will return to Roussillon?' he asked.

'Yes, he will likely return to France. And with the sad news of his wife, who left for pilgrimage but has now passed away, he will feel as if he is free from that tie.' The group continued to sadly discuss Helena's story. After a while Bertram returned, seeming

pleased with himself.

'Well, I've had one productive night! I have dealt with a month's worth of tasks in one evening. I've mourned a wife, written to my mother, said goodbye to the duke, entertained fans and won over a new love,' he said. 'Now, what about Parolles? Has he revealed his true self?' The soldiers looked at each other, smiling, and then led Bertram to him.

Parolles was still blindfolded, and sat moaning in the corner.

‘I have told the truth. Please let me go!’ he begged. The leader, who was acting as translator, told him there were a few more questions about the number of horses and men the duke’s army

had. The answers flowed from Parolles like a raging river, with no attempt to hide the truth. Next, the leader questioned Parolles about his captain and the duke. Without hesitation, Parolles launched into a string of insults. He began with the captain. 'He is terrible, and the duke thinks he is a poor officer!' He swiftly proceeded to offend them all. Bertram and the soldiers watched in disbelief, their faces filled with disgust.

'If we spare your life, will you betray the Florentines?' the leader tested. Bertram took a deep breath in and waited.

'Yes, and the Captain Count Roussillon,' Parolles immediately responded. Bertram threw his hands up in despair, feeling embarrassed that he had ever trusted this man. They let Parolles sit and wait for a while, before deciding it was time.

The men formed a semi-circle around Parolles. 'Before we decide your fate, you may want to say goodbye to your friends,' the leader said, slowly removing Parolles's blindfold. He blinked a few times, adjusting to the light. Each of the men greeted Captain Parolles. His face dropped and his eyes widened in shock.

He hung his head low as the men departed, leaving him alone to wallow in his embarrassment.

Helena, Diana and her mother were swiftly travelling to France to explain everything that had happened to the king. 'They think I'm dead, you know?' Helena said, amused. 'And my husband is now hurrying home.' She turned to the women, her words heartfelt and full of gratitude. 'I am so grateful for your help.'

The other two women smiled and reassured her that they were there for her, no matter what. 'We shall sort things out with Bertram and all will be well,' Helena insisted. 'After all, all's well that ends well,' she added, feeling optimistic about how the plan would unfold.

Chapter Eight

Tears streamed down the countess's cheeks. She had heard the false news of Helena's death and felt as though she had lost her own child. Lafeu consoled her, acknowledging Helena's uniqueness and expressing his own sense of loss.

After several minutes of waiting

for the countess to calm herself, Lafeu carefully shared a plan he had discussed with the king. 'Now that your son is returning home wifeless, I suggested that perhaps my daughter would be a suitable match. The king approved. What do you think of this, countess?' For a moment the countess collected her thoughts. After a long silence, she agreed, forcing a smile and wishing them every happiness.

A sudden announcement snapped the countess out of her thoughts. Her son had just arrived home.

The three women were tired. They had been travelling day and night to reach the king in Marseille. Helena apologised for perhaps the seventeenth time that hour, watching with guilt as the elderly mother pushed on. A gentleman appeared on a horse not far behind them. Helena waved him down. 'Please can we ask for your assistance? We are looking for the king,' she said politely.

'The king is not here. He left this morning for Roussillon. I'm

going there now,' the gentleman told them.

'Oh! We have travelled all this way for nothing!' cried Diana's mother.

'That's okay. We shall go to Roussillon,' Helena decided. 'Please can you give this to him, as you'll get there before us,' she asked, passing him a letter.

The gentleman agreed and continued riding.

Back in Roussillon, the king had arrived. The countess greeted him warmly. After sharing their sadness at the loss of Helena, the countess apologised for her son's behaviour and asked for forgiveness. The king put his hand up to stop her. 'I have put it behind me. Don't get me wrong, there were times I wanted to avenge that sweet girl's death,' the

king confessed. 'I have felt anger and sadness, but I know I must move on and forgive.'

Lafeu joined them. 'I have to say, although he wronged so many, the person he hurt the most was himself – losing such a remarkable wife.' The countess and the king nodded in agreement.

'Bring him to me,' the king instructed a nearby gentleman. 'Tell him not to ask for my forgiveness, but to approach me as a stranger.'

Bertram entered the room a few minutes later. He appeared

somewhat sheepish and was keeping his head held low. He approached the king and slowly made eye contact. Bertram opened

his mouth to speak, but the king instantly cut him off. 'It is forgotten. I don't want to discuss it further. I've realised life is short and we must move on,' he finished. Bertram nodded and looked at the ground.

'Now, do you remember Lafeu's daughter?' the king enquired, gesturing towards Lafeu and swiftly changing the subject.

Bertram nodded. 'Yes. I do remember her. I used to want to marry her!'

Bertram's words seemed to please the king. 'Well, that is good news. I've agreed for you to marry her. So, send a token of your love and let's arrange another wedding,' he concluded.

Bertram took off the ring that Diana had given him in exchange for his, and handed it to Lafeu. The instant Lafeu saw it, his face changed. 'This is Helena's ring!' he said angrily. 'The last time I saw her, she was wearing it!' he shouted, his eyes wide as he waited for Bertram to explain.

Chapter Nine

The room's atmosphere had changed. People shifted uncomfortably at the scene that was unfolding. Lafeu gave the ring to the king, who twisted it onto his finger. 'This is mine! I gave it to Helena and told her to send it to me if she ever needed my help!' His pleasant expression was replaced with fury.

Bertram protested, 'It is not hers; you are mistaken! A girl in Florence gave it to me. She threw it out her window, believing we were engaged. But I told her I would never marry her!'

'Enough!' the king bellowed. 'I know it was hers! I fear the worst. She swore she would never take it off unless she was in danger, and now here it is and she is gone!' he raged. He called the guards to take Bertram away. 'We will find out the truth,' he warned.

As Bertram was escorted from the room, another gentleman

entered timidly. 'I'm sorry if it's a bad time, but I have a letter from a lady in Florence who's tried many times to find you.'

The flustered king took the letter and started reading:

'I was fooled. After promising many times that he would marry me when his wife passed, the Count of Roussillon, now a widower, broke his vows to me. Please grant me justice, Diana.' The king frowned. 'Is she here?' he asked the gentleman, who nodded back. 'Send her up!'

Lafeu threw his hands in the air. 'Forget it! I forbid my daughter to marry this vile man.' The countess

widower

A man whose wife has died.

held her head, with no defence to offer for her son's behaviour.

Diana and her mother were shown into the room. Bertram, still by the door, turned away. 'Do you know this woman?' the king demanded.

'I might. But she is nothing to me,' he replied dismissively.

'Your wife is nothing to you?' Diana retorted, handing Bertram's ring to his mother. The countess looked at the ring, speechless.

'For six generations this has been in my family. This is proof she's telling the truth,' she confirmed, shaking her head sadly.

Bertram shook his head in disagreement, trying to deny the situation.

'He can confirm it is true,' Diana said, pointing to a sheepish Parolles, who'd snuck into the room. 'Did Bertram not promise to marry me?' she insisted.

Parolles kept his gaze on the floor. 'He did,' he said feebly. Bertram scoffed, looking at him angrily.

'And there's something else,' Diana admitted. 'It wasn't my ring to give. I was acting on behalf of a friend. Someone who has also been wronged!' she explained. The king was overwhelmed, and the countess looked like she might faint.

The door opened, and there stood Helena. The king tried to speak but no words came out.

'It is me,' she confirmed, addressing the questioning looks.

Bertram rushed to her. 'Helena, please forgive me,' he begged. 'We have exchanged rings and fulfilled the terms of our marriage, so will you now be my husband?' she asked.

Bertram looked at the king. 'I don't know what's happened. But if she explains, I will love her dearly,' he promised.

The room's atmosphere changed once again. This time it was filled with joy and kindness. The countess hugged Helena lovingly. The king promised he would take care of Diana and her mother. Lafeu watched on with teary eyes.

'Come, Helena. There's a story to be told and we want to hear everything,' said the king, overjoyed at her return. They gathered round as Helena retold the whole tale.